4

Four

5

Five

6

Six

Ten

10

11

Eleven

Twelve

12

Peter Rabbit's
1 2 3

With new reproductions from the original illustrations by
BEATRIX POTTER

F. WARNE & Co ™

How many little rabbits,
eating radishes?

"First he ate some lettuces and some French beans,
and then he ate some radishes."

From *The Tale of Peter Rabbit*

2

How many yellow stockings,
for Sally Henny-penny?

"Oh, that's a pair of stockings belonging
to Sally Henny-penny."

From *The Tale of Mrs. Tiggy-Winkle*

3

How many kittens,
playing in the dust?

"Once upon a time, there were three little kittens,
and their names were Mittens, Tom Kitten and Moppet."

From *The Tale of Tom Kitten*

How many guinea-pigs,
going gardening?

"We have a little garden,
A garden of our own,
And every day we water there
The seeds that we have sown."
From *Cecily Parsley's Nursery Rhymes*

How many mice,
snippeting and snappeting?

"There was a snippeting of scissors, and a snappeting of thread;
and little mouse voices sang loudly and gaily."

From *The Tailor of Gloucester*

6

How many fat Flopsy Bunnies?

" 'One, two, three, four, five, six leetle fat rabbits!'
repeated Mr. McGregor, counting on his fingers."

From *The Tale of The Flopsy Bunnies*

How many red squirrels,
with the old brown owl?

"Nutkin danced up and down like a *sunbeam*,
but still Old Brown said nothing at all."

From *The Tale of Squirrel Nutkin*

8

How many piglets,
feeding from a trough?

"Four little boy pigs and four little girl pigs
are too many altogether."

From *The Tale of Pigling Bland*

9

How many mice
round the supper table?

"The dinner was of eight courses;
not much of anything, but truly elegant."

From *The Tale of Johnny Town-Mouse*

10

How many mice,
living in the shoe?

"I think if she lived in a little shoe-house –
That little old woman was surely a mouse!"
From *Appley Dapply's Nursery Rhymes*

How many birds
in the hen coop?

"The owner came with a lantern and a hamper
to catch six fowls to take to market in the morning."

From *The Tale of Pigling Bland*

12

How many animals
round the notice-board?

Endpaper design

How many rabbits can you see?

How many squirrels can you see?

How many mice can you see?

"Once upon a time there was a village shop.
The name over the window was 'Ginger and Pickles'."

From *The Tale of Ginger and Pickles*

How many shop-keepers
behind the counter?

How many customers
in front of the counter?

"The counter inside was a convenient height for rabbits."

From *The Tale of Ginger and Pickles*

How many rats inside the meal sack?

How many rats outside the meal sack?

Endpaper design for *The Tale of Samuel Whiskers*

FREDERICK WARNE

Published by the Penguin Group
27 Wrights Lane, London W8 5TZ, England
Penguin Books USA Inc., 375 Hudson Street, New York, New York 10014, USA
Penguin Books Australia Ltd, Ringwood, Victoria, Australia
Penguin Books Canada Ltd, 10 Alcorn Avenue, Toronto, Ontario, Canada M4V 3B2
Penguin Books (N.Z.) Ltd, 182-190 Wairau Road, Auckland 10, New Zealand

Penguin Books Ltd, Registered Offices: Harmondsworth, Middlesex, England

First published by Frederick Warne & Co. 1987
Reissued 1998

ISBN 0 7232 3424 8

Printed and bound in Singapore

One

Two

Three

Seven

Eight

Nine